For my very own Dramatic Duo: Finn & Seán – E.C.

To Egbert, my imaginary friend. And to Michael, my real one – O. J.

First published in hardback in Great Britain by HarperCollins Children's Books in 2015
First published in paperback in 2016

1 3 5 7 9 10 8 6 4 2

ISBN: 978-0-00-812616-2

HarperCollins Children's Books is a division of HarperCollins Publishers Ltd.

Text copyright © Eoin Colfer, Artemis Fowl Ltd 2015
Illustrations copyright © Oliver Jeffers 2015, 2016

Visit our website at: www.harpercollins.co.uk

Printed and bound in China

Imaginary
FRED

EOIN COLFER
OLIVER JEFFERS

HarperCollins *Children's Books*

Headaches are a pain. A bee sting hurts even more. But there is one thing that's worse than getting stung on the head by a bee on a rainy day, and that is... loneliness.

Being alone is no fun.

The first five minutes are OK, but it's downhill from there. And if you're alone, you're alone. It's not as if you can wish a friend to life.

Usually this is true. You can wish and wish until your hair stands on end, but no imaginary friend will appear.

Unless...

...the conditions are just right,
and if you add a little electricity,

or luck,

or even magic,

then an imaginary friend might appear just when you need one.

An imaginary friend like Fred.

Fred floated like a feather in the wind until a lonely little child wished for him.

Fred was
always happy
to be
summoned.

And he tried really hard to be the best imaginary friend
he could be.

He dressed up.

Dressed down.

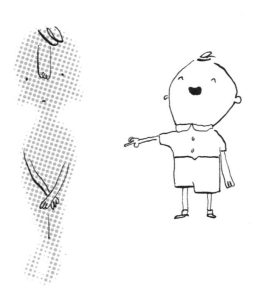

Played ball.

Became a ball.

And did whatever else his real friend wanted
to do, without once complaining.

But no matter how hard Fred tried, the same thing happened every
time. One day, his friend would find a real friend in the real world.

A friend who did not have to be ignored
when grown-ups were around.

When this day came,
as it always did, Fred
would feel himself fade.

Usually by lunchtime on the second day, Fred would be mostly invisible, and by bedtime on the fourth day there would barely be a scrap of Fred left, just enough for the wind to catch and whisk him into the sky...

...where Fred would
stay until someone new
wished for him.

Fred was glad that his friends found other real friends to play with, but sometimes he wished he had a friend who would need him forever.

He dreamed of a friend
who liked reading, music
and drama like he did.

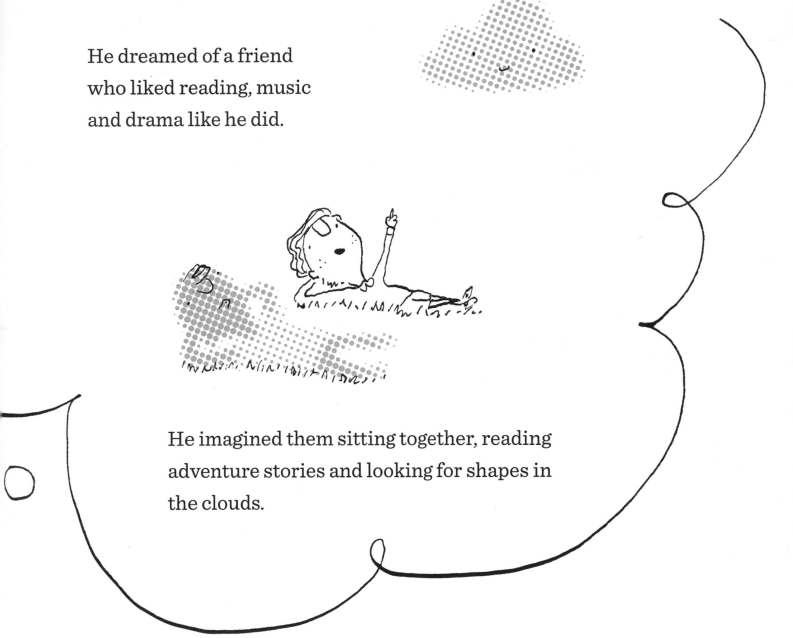

He imagined them sitting together, reading
adventure stories and looking for shapes in
the clouds.

This was Fred's dream.

And one day...

a lonely boy called Sam wished hard for a
friend, when the conditions were perfect.

Fred appeared and soon realised that Sam
was the friend he had been dreaming of.

Fred never had so much fun. Sam loved to read, just like Fred, and was most upset if he didn't get through at least one book per day.

When they weren't reading, Sam and Fred would try to understand how the toilet worked,

they'd listen to music on Sam's dad's sound system, which had thirteen speakers,

or they would write plays and act them out for Sam's parents.

But even though every morning brought new delights, Fred couldn't help thinking that every evening brought them closer to the day when Sam wouldn't need him any more. And that would be the saddest day of his imaginary life.

So Fred decided that he would enjoy every single moment with Sam until that time came.

The two friends pretended to be French and studied mime.
They made Japanese masks, practised their classical instruments
and planned their own comic book. They called themselves
the Dramatic Duo.

But one day, Sam came home late from a party and Fred felt a nervous flutter in his imaginary tummy.

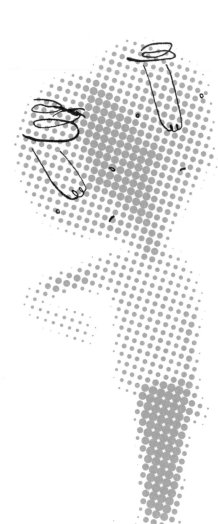

Was this the beginning of the end?

Was he headed back into the sky?

Fred checked his arm and thought that maybe he had faded a little already.

When Sam came home, he had
an excited look in his eyes.

A look Fred had seen before.

"I made a new friend," Sam told him. "She's a girl called Sammi, which is funny because I'm called Sam. She loves to read and has written and illustrated her own comic book series. You're going to love her, Fred."

Fred thought he probably would love Sammi, if he were able to stay around long enough to meet her.

"But don't worry," Sam said. "Just because I met Sammi doesn't mean I don't need you. You're still my main man." In Fred's experience there was only room in a heart for one best friend.

"I will always be your friend," Fred said. "Just promise that you won't forget me."
"I promise," said Sam, and he meant it.

The next morning, Sam was gone when Fred woke up and there was a note on his pillow:

I AM MEETING
SAMMi to
BRAINSTORM OUR
COMIC BOOK.
BACK LATER.
Your Pal,
SAM

Comic book? thought Fred. *That was our idea. Me and Sam.* Fred checked his arm again. Definite fading this time.

When Sam came home several hours later, Fred called an emergency meeting of the Dramatic Duo.

"OK, Sam," he said. "I want to prepare you for what's coming. In a day or two, I will disappear. It's not your fault. It's just that now that you have a real friend, you don't need me any more. The best thing you can do is let me go without making a scene."

Sam did make a scene.

He swore he would never let Fred go.

But the next day, Sam left the house early again to meet
with Sammi, and Fred was left behind.

I can see through
my hand now,
thought Fred.

When Sam returned
home later that day,
he brought Sammi with him.
Sammi wore round glasses that
made her eyes seem huge. She pulled
a cello case behind her on a trolley, and carried an art bag so
she could work on her comic book whenever an idea struck.

Sam introduced them. "Sammi, meet Fred. Fred, meet Sammi."

This is a waste of time, thought Fred. *Only people with an imaginary friend can see an imaginary friend.*

But Sammi stuck her hand out in exactly the right direction and said, "Pleased to meet you, Fred."

Fred was surprised. He had never been visible to two people before. He shook Sammi's hand.

"I know you're worried I don't need you any more," said Sam. "But you're wrong. I need you more than ever."

"Why?" asked Fred. "Why do you need me now? You've got Sammi."

"Two reasons," said Sam. "First: I never want to let you go."

Fred thought he would cry, and that was only reason number one.

"And reason number two?" he asked.

"Tell him," said Sammi, elbowing Sam the way friends do.

"OK," said Sam. "Reason number two is that we need you to be in our quartet."

Fred was confused. "Quartet means four," he said. "There are only three of us."

"Aha!" said Sam, like a great detective. "That's where you're wrong."

"Yes," said Sammi, clapping her hands. "You're wrong because there *are* four of us."

Sammi stepped to one side and Fred saw a small
girl with a violin case, and a smile that made him
want to smile, too.

"This is Frieda," said Sammi.
"Hi, Fred," said Frieda, waving her hand. "Sam's told us
all about you. I hope we can be friends."

Sammi has an imaginary friend! Fred realised, and
as he waved back he noticed that his hand seemed
absolutely solid. Not see-through at all.

Frieda set her violin case on the floor and opened it.
"We need to practise," she said. "Or we'll never get to
Carnegie Hall."
Sammi rolled her eyes. "Frieda is so strict," she said
to Fred. "But you'll get used to it in a couple of years."

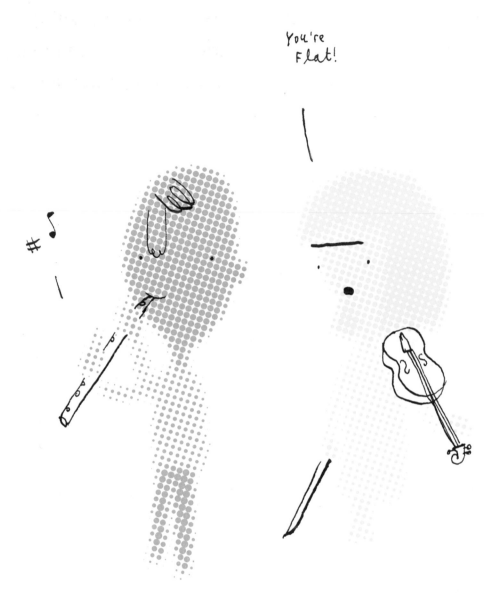

Fred did get used to it. He quite enjoyed being told what to do by Frieda with her dazzling smile.

The four friends spent all their spare time together, having violin battles, reading comic books, practising plumbing, pretending to be French and arguing over what they would call their quartet.

They eventually settled on the Quarrelling Quartet,
which they all agreed was the perfect name.
The quartet made their debut at the School
Christmas Concert, much to the confusion
of the audience.

But then something interesting happened.
The older they grew, the less time the
four friends spent together.

Sam and Sammi, it seemed, preferred graphic novels to music, and they left the quartet to concentrate on their comic book series.

Carnegie Hall was eventually
played. Not as a quartet, however,
but as a duo.

Again, much to the confusion of the audience.

And this, dear friends, is the interesting thing that happened: even though they didn't see their human friends much any more, Fred and Frieda did not begin to fade, nor get swept back up into the sky like they had so many times before.

Instead, they stuck around being imaginary friends to each other.
They became quite famous in the imaginary community, and
a statue was commissioned to be erected in the sky above their
imaginary house.

As this was the first case of its kind, imaginary scientists spent years trying to figure out how it had happened.

Eventually they
concluded that
friendship is friendship.
Imaginary or not,
the same laws apply.

The statue should have disappeared
every time a gust of wind came along.

But it never did.